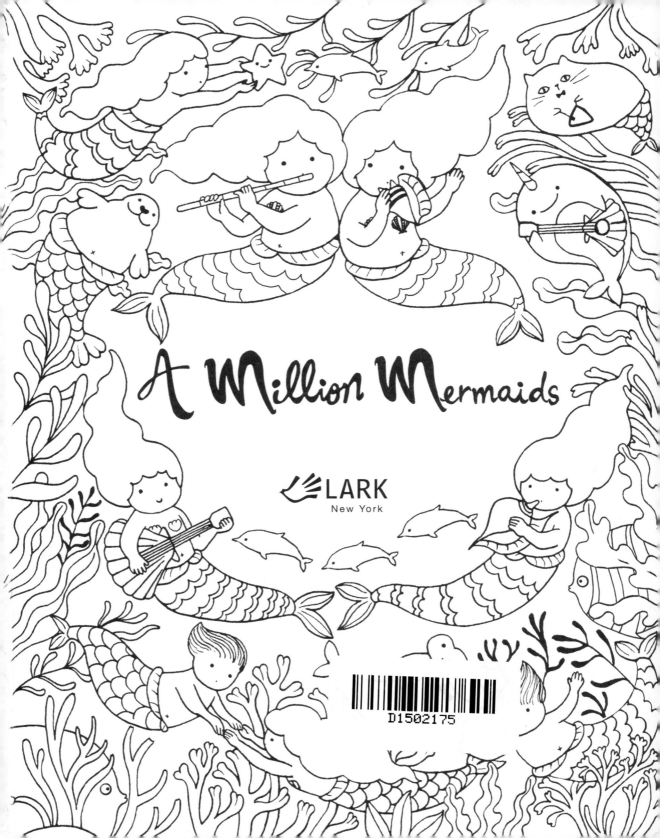

A Million Mermaids

LARK
New York

LARK
New York

An Imprint of Sterling Publishing Co., Inc.
1166 Avenue of the Americas
New York, NY 10036

ISBN 978-1-4547-1115-5

Distributed in Canada by Sterling Publishing
c/o Canadian Manda Group, 664 Annette Street
Toronto, Ontario M6S 2C8, Canada

For information about custom editions, special sales, and premium and corporate purchases,
please contact Sterling Special Sales at 800-805-5489 or specialsales@sterlingpublishing.com.

Manufactured in China

Lot#:
2 4 6 8 10 9 7 5 3 1
04/20

sterlingpublishing.com/larkcrafts

Illustrated by

Lulu Mayo